For Elizabeth
and the Oakwood years
—J.H.

For Cori and Kaitlyn; and Ricky and Emma
—T.C.K.

Published simultaneously in Canada.
Manufactured in China by South China Printing Co. Ltd.
Designed by Gina DiMassi. Text set in Font Soup Catalan.
The art was done in colored pencil, chalk pastels, and collage on Canson paper.
Library of Congress Cataloging-in-Publication Data
Harper, Jessica. Four boys named Jordan / Jessica Harper ;
illustrated by Tara Calahan King.   p. cm. Summary: Four Jordans
in one third-grade classroom cause chaos and confusion
for teacher and students alike. [1. Names, Personal—Fiction.
2. Schools—Fiction. 3. Stories in rhyme.] I. King, Tara Calahan, ill. II. Title.
PZ8.3.H219   Fo 2004   [E]—dc21   2002155719
ISBN 0-399-23711-9
10 9 8 7 6 5 4 3 2 1
First Impression

# FOUR BOYS NAMED JORDAN

Jordan N.

JORDAN S.

Jordan P.

Jordan F.

Jessica Harper

illustrated by

Tara Calahan King

G. P. Putnam's Sons
New York

My name is Elizabeth and I am in third grade.
We're studying Egyptians and those pyramids they made.
Sometimes I think Egyptian life was pretty complicated,
but next to life in my classroom, it's highly overrated!!

GET THIS:

I sit there, at table 6, with Zachary and Max.

It's fine, except when Max and Zack get giggling attacks.

Costumes
Box #2

But you will not believe what's going on at table 3:
There's Jordan S. on one side, next to him is Jordan P.!
But that's not all, there's also Jordan N. at table 8!
And just when you begin to think
you've finally got them straight . . .

A new kid came to class today.
He walked in the door
and said his name was . . .
can you guess?
He's Jordan number four!

Four boys named Jordan!
Four Jordans in a row!
How many Jordans are there on the planet,
do you know?
Here a Jordan, there a Jordan,
careful, you might miss one!
Of all the classrooms here on Earth,
why did they all pick this one?!

Jordan N.

JORDAN S.

Jordan P.

Jordan F.

Zack

The teacher asks if Jordan's present.
Four boys answer,

"YES!"

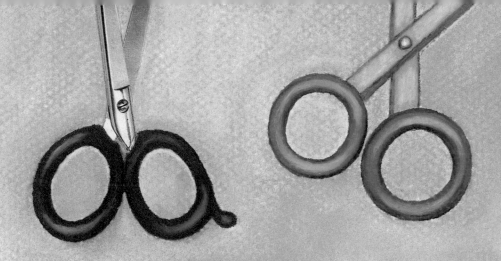

Say, "Jordan, pass the scissors,"
and you'll end up with four pairs.

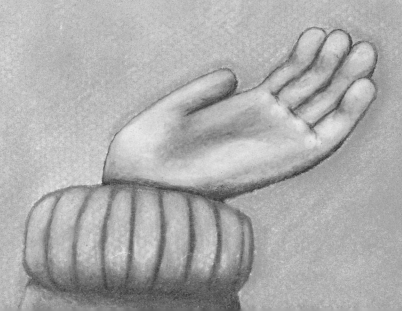

Say, "Jordan, there's a test today."

Four voices say, **"Who cares?"**

At recess if you try to talk to some Jordan or other,
you'll only get in trouble, so I really wouldn't bother.
Just say, "Hi, Jordan." You will get,
"Which Jordan do you mean?
The tall one or the small one
or the one that's in-between?"

"Do you mean me?"

"Or me?"

"Or me? Please try
to be specific."

"Don't talk to that one,
talk to me. I'm really
quite terrific!"

"Oh, no, you're not!"

"Oh, yes, I am!"

You see? Don't even try it.
Be friendly to a Jordan
and you start a minor riot!

I hope the next new kid we get
is named something like Harry.
I'd even settle for a Robert. I could live with Larry.
If we keep getting Jordans, soon the Jordan population
will increase until this classroom is a Jordan nation!

We got a new girl in our class.
Her name? You'll never guess.
Unless you guess the J-word,
and then I'd answer, "Yes."